THE TITANIUM NINJA

ADAPTED BY KATE HOWARD

SCHOLASTIC INC.

ISBN 978-0-545-66386-1

LEGO, the LEGO logo, NINJAGO, the Brick and Knob configurations and the Minifigure are trademarks of the LEGO Group. © 2015 the LEGO Group. Produced by Scholastic Inc. under license from the LEGO Group.
Published by Scholastic Inc. SCHOLASTIC and associated logos are trademarks and/or registered trademarks of Scholastic Inc.

12 11 10 9 8 7 6 5 4 3   15 16 17 18 19 20/0
Printed in the U.S.A.   40

First printing, January 2015

THE GOLDEN ARMOR

"The Golden Armor will *sssoon* be ready for your evil bidding, my Dark *Lordsssship*," Pythor told the Overlord.

The two villains watched as the Golden Weapons were melted down. Once the Overlord put on the Golden Armor, he would be all-powerful.

"Yes! Yes! Behold the beginnings of the Golden Master!" cried the Overlord.

Meanwhile, the ninja—Jay, Cole, Zane, Kai, and Lloyd—were losing hope. They had gone into space to protect the Golden Weapons, but they had failed—and they were stranded.

"I should've never given up my Golden Power," moaned Lloyd. "Now the Overlord has all he needs to become the Golden Master."

"Search for the power within, and then realize the greatness within each other," Sensei Wu advised them.

"We can get off this planet!" Lloyd said. "Our ship may not fly, but she has the metal we need to build a new one. And Zane knows space better than anyone. He could get us home."

"Kai's fire power can weld it," said Zane.

"Cole's manpower can do the heavy lifting," said Kai.

"And Jay has enough electricity and nerd knowledge to make a spacecraft," said Cole.

Jay grinned. "Hey! This could actually work!"

The ninja got to work. Each used his elemental power to build a new ship. "Let's fire this thing up and see if she'll fly," said Kai.

As a robot ninja, Zane had special powers to give the ship power. He plugged his heart into the rocket, and the ship blasted off.

"Let's go home, fellas," said Lloyd.

THE GOLDEN MASTER

Back in Ninjago™, the Overlord's Golden Armor was ready. Finally, he had the power to take charge!

"Bow to your Golden Master!" cried the Overlord. Security mechs fired at him, but it was no use. He swatted them away like flies. "You've heard of the power of the First Spinjitzu Master. Now witness the power of the last!"

The people of New Ninjago City fought back against the Overlord.

"They *refussse* to bow, Golden *Massster*. They are hoping the ninja will return," said Pythor.

The Overlord cackled. "Don't they know there are no ninja?"

But the Overlord was wrong. "Look!" cried a man fleeing down the street. "It's the ninja!"

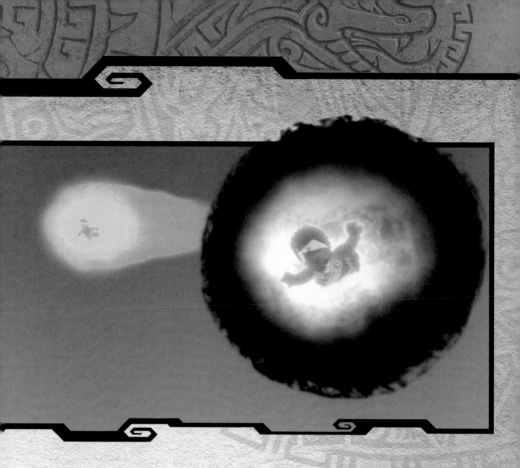

Pythor gasped. "They've returned? But how?"

The ninja's ship had taken them almost all the way back to Ninjago. Now, using their elemental shields for protection, they were hurtling through the air toward New Ninjago City.

"If the ninja are what give the people hope, then we'll crush them. Prepare for battle!" the Overlord screamed.

Using his Golden Power, the Overlord created a barrier out of the buildings around him. Soon, he'd created a wall around New Ninjago City. He was ready to take over!

NINJA STEALTH ATTACK

Just outside the city, the ninja met up with
Nya, Pixal, Sensei Wu, and Sensei Garmadon.

"It's good to have you back," said Sensei Wu.

The ninja and their friends headed toward
New Ninjago City. But they stopped short
outside the city.

"That's not a city . . . It's a fortress!" Jay cried.

Suddenly, an image of the inventor Cyrus Borg popped up on the team's monitors. "Ninja, I have found refuge within the Temple of Fortitude."

"The Overlord used the Temple as a stronghold during the Stone Wars," Sensei Wu said.

"Its seal of protection can resist the Golden Power," said Sensei Garmadon.

"I have a device that could defeat the Overlord," Borg continued.

"We have to get to that Temple!" said Lloyd.

Cole charged straight through the buildings, leaving a path for Jay, Pixal, Wu, and Garmadon. Kai and the others tried to drive over the walls.

As they climbed, Nya asked, "Is that wall getting higher?"

"The Overlord's turf, his rules," explained Zane.

"The Temple's up ahead," yelled Garmadon.

Zooming through the city, the ninja and their friends used their weapons to protect innocent people from attacking Nindroids.

Suddenly, Nya's vehicle was hit. "Nya's down!" Kai cried.

"Go!" screamed Nya as she faced off against General Cryptor. "I can take care of myself."

Just then, an explosion threw the ninja off their vehicles. The Overlord was right behind them!

The Golden Master began to use Spinjitzu like the ninja had never seen. He was a giant tornado, whirling toward them as they ran for the Temple. And he was getting closer!

The ninja sped through the city toward the Temple, where Wu and Garmadon were waiting. As soon as they rushed in, Wu cried, "Brother, now!" He and Garmadon slammed the doors.

A powerful shield wrapped around the Temple. The ninja were safe—for now.

PLAN OF ATTACK

Cyrus Borg was waiting inside.

"You said you had a weapon that could stop the Overlord?" asked Lloyd.

Borg nodded. "I do. It's my most protected secret." He showed them a secure box.

"A pill?" Jay said, lifting an eyebrow.

"Not just any pill. A nano pill," Borg said. "If swallowed, it miniaturizes you."

"You've made a shrinking pill?" said Zane.

"Lemme get this straight," said Kai. "You want us to get close to a guy who could make us toast . . . and you want us to give him a pill?"

"Brother, do you remember when we were on the same team as children?" said Garmadon. "I threw a mean curve ball, and your stick could thread the needle. We never lost."

Sensei Wu nodded. "Get us close, ninja, and we'll give the Golden Master his medicine."

IS ALL HOPE LOST?

As the ninja planned inside the Temple, the Overlord was destroying the city around him.

"The people are *losssing* hope," hissed Pythor. "*Sssoon* they will bow to you, Golden *Massster*."

The Overlord pulled power lines off their poles. He flung them through the air, creating a giant web. Soon he would be unstoppable!

"Are we sure this is going to protect us?" Kai asked, looking at the stone armor Sensei Wu had given them.

Garmadon nodded. "If the Overlord's Stone Warriors used this against the First Spinjitzu Master, we can use it against the same powers."

"There is only enough armor for them," Cyrus Borg told Pixal. "We will have to go without."

"You take it," Zane told Pixal.

Pixal shook her head. "No, you are vital for this mission. Don't worry about me. I shall see you again."

Suddenly, the Temple wall burst open, and Nindroids swarmed in.

Then, someone blasted them out of the way. It was Nya!

"Better late than never!" she shouted. "Go get 'em, ninja!"

GO, NINGA, GO!

The ninja ran across rooftops, dodging the Overlord's attacks.

"The armor's working!" Cole shouted.

"Keep going!" said Jay. "We have to take the heat off the senseis!"

The ninja dashed toward the Overlord. They blasted through his walls and barriers.

"My powers!" moaned the Overlord. "They aren't working! They won't stop coming!"

"We'll never get close enough," groaned Kai. The Golden Master loomed above them, perched on his golden web.

But Sensei Garmadon wasn't worried. "We won't need to. Are you ready to thread the needle, Brother?"

"Let's show them what old timers can do," said Sensei Wu.

Holding the pill in his hand, Garmadon jumped onto the Overlord's web and bounced high. Then Sensei Wu jumped onto his back, and Garmadon hurled his brother into the air.

With a mighty spin, Sensei Wu whacked the pill with his staff. It flew through the air . . . straight toward the Overlord's open mouth!

At the last minute, Pythor leaped into the air—and caught the pill in his own mouth! The last of the Anacondrai screamed as he shrunk down to worm-size. "*What'sss* happening to me?! No!"

The ninja were crushed. Their plan had failed.

"That's it?" mocked the Overlord. "That's all you've got?!"

One by one, the Overlord caught the ninja in his webbing. "All hope is lost!"

NINJA NEVER QUIT

But the Overlord couldn't catch Zane.

"Hope is not lost!" the Ninja of Ice cried. He grabbed hold of the Overlord's Golden Armor. "Let my friends go!"

"The Golden Weapons are too powerful for you to behold," cackled the Overlord.

But Zane held fast. "Your days are over!"

The others watched as the Overlord's—and Zane's—powers began to fail.

"Let go of him, Zane!" Kai shouted. "What is he doing?"

"He's protecting us," Sensei Wu said.

Zane held on, even as the Overlord's Golden Power tore his body apart. "This is about family. Ninja never quit—go, ninja, go!" he cried.

"Let me go, you fool!" the Overlord screamed.

"No, Zane, no!" Jay cried.

A bright light burst out of Zane's heart. He and the Golden Master froze over. A moment later, they exploded into icy shards.

The Overlord was gone.
And so was Zane.

THE TITANIUM NINJA

When he fought the Golden Master, Zane's
eart had broken.

The other ninja's hearts were broken, too.
hey had lost their brother. They gathered to
emember the fallen ninja.

"Zane was the perfect balance between us
nd technology," Cyrus Borg said. "Technology
an improve our lives, but so can people. He
aved us all." Borg pulled a sheet off a statue. "I
resent to you all: the Titanium Ninja."

Kai stood up. "Everyone wonders what powered Zane. I like to think it was brotherhood. Because he powered me. And he'll still power me as his memory lives on. Ninja never quit, and ninja will never be forgotten. Wherever you are, Zane, you'll always be one of us."

As Kai finished speaking, it began to snow. Somewhere, somehow, Zane was watching over them.